THE SURPRISE DOLL

THE SUR

STORY BY **Morrell Gipson**

ILLUSTRATIONS BY **Steffie Lerch**

60th Anniversary Edition

Purple House Press · KENTUCKY

Also available from Purple House Press
Mr. Bear Squash-You-All-Flat by Morrell Gipson

Published by
Purple House Press
PO Box 787, Cynthiana, KY 41031

Find more Classic Books for Kids at purplehousepress.com

Printed in Korea by PACOM
2 3 4 5 6 7 8 9 10

The Surprise Doll

Mary lived in a little house on the side of a hill, right over the ocean.

Mary had big brown eyes, a nose that went up like this,
eyebrows that went up like that, hair as yellow as
butter, and cheeks that were pink from the sun and wind.
And when she smiled, she smiled all over her face.

Mary's father was a sea captain. He took long trips across the ocean in his ship. From her window Mary waved *goodbye* to him when he sailed away. And from her window she waved *hello* to him when he came sailing back. Six times he came back with a doll for Mary, so she had six dolls, from six different countries across the ocean.

First, there was Susan,
who had cheeks that were pink from the sun and wind

She came from England.

Sonya, who had a nose
that went up like this.

She came from Russia.

Teresa, who had big brown eyes.

She came from Italy.

Lang Po, who had eyebrows that went up like that.

She came from China.

Katrinka, who had hair as yellow as butter.

She came from Holland.

And Marie,
who smiled all over her face.

She came from France.

These were Mary's six dolls,
and she loved them very much. But one day she said
to her father, "I have a doll for every day in the week
but Sunday. Please, won't you bring me a Sunday doll?"

Her father shook his head so hard that his sea cap fell off. "No, my dear," he said. "Six dolls are enough for any little girl." But they weren't enough for Mary!

So one morning Mary hopped out of bed,

dressed herself,

dressed her dolls,

put them all in her little red wagon,

went out of her little house and down the hill,

and through the woods,

and over the bridge.

Finally
she came to the
shop of the Dollmaker.

The Dollmaker was working away, busy as a bee, but he stopped when Mary and her dolls came in.

Mary said, "I am Mary, and these
are my six dolls, Susan and Sonya and Teresa and
Lang Po and Katrinka and Marie. I came to see you
because I need a seventh doll, a doll for Sunday."

The Dollmaker looked at Mary. Then he looked at
her dolls. Then he looked at Mary again. And he
gave a great big jolly laugh. "Certainly, I will make
you a Sunday doll," he said. "But you will have to
leave your six dolls with me while I work. In seven
days it will be ready. And be prepared for a surprise
when you see it. Oh, yes, a real surprise." And he
chuckled as he went back to work.

So Mary left her dolls at the Dollmaker's, and took her empty wagon over the bridge and through the woods and up the hill and back home again.

She counted the days off on her calendar. It was a
long time to be without any dolls at all!

And in seven days she went back to see the Dollmaker.

There were Susan and Sonya and Teresa and Lang Po and Katrinka and Marie. And *there* was Mary's new doll. It was a Surprise Doll! Can you guess why?

Well, the new doll had cheeks that were pink from the sun and wind, like Susan *and* like Mary.

And a nose that went up like this, like Sonya *and* like Mary.

And eyebrows that went up like that, like Lang Po *and* like Mary.

And eyes that were big and brown, like Teresa *and* like Mary.

And hair that was as yellow as butter, like Katrinka *and* like Mary.

And a smile all over her face, like Marie *and* like Mary.

The Surprise Doll looked a little bit like every one of
Mary's other dolls, and JUST LIKE MARY!

What a happy day that was for Mary. She named her Sunday Surprise Doll, Mary Jane.
And just like Mary, Mary Jane came from America.
Mary gave a big tea party to celebrate!

Purple House Press

Classic Books for Kids

purplehousepress.com